Silas W. Mitchell

Philip Vernon

A tale in prose and verse

Silas W. Mitchell

Philip Vernon
A tale in prose and verse

ISBN/EAN: 9783337072346

Printed in Europe, USA, Canada, Australia, Japan

Cover: Foto ©Andreas Hilbeck / pixelio.de

More available books at **www.hansebooks.com**

PHILIP VERNON

A TALE
IN PROSE AND VERSE

BY

S. WEIR MITCHELL
M.D., LL.D., HARVARD

NEW YORK
THE CENTURY CO.
1895

PHILIP VERNON

THE INN

JULY 21, 1588

WHEN Bess was queen and the Bishop of Rome and
the King of Spain were troubling our England, the
cowls were many in the land, and knew how to pull
the lamb-skins well around them.

One of these wolves, of a summer morning, walked,
halting a little, to and fro under the great oaks between the Vernon Arms and the road. His sheep's
clothing was a burgher's gray hose and doublet; but
he was not right, red English, having of late come
out of Spain, yellow-cheeked and lean. He looked
down the highway to the bridge, and then with his
eyes followed the river curves to the sea, whence, he
smiled to think, the great Armada would come, in
time to help certain wicked schemes, and set the
cowls again in high places. Then, less pleased, he cast
looks at a gallant in blue with yellow points, who sat
at a table a little way from the inn. This gentle had
a good leg and was high-colored and young. At times
he drummed on the table, or uneasily cast down his

cap, and once half drew his sword, then presently, as
if impatient, drove it back into its sheath. But whether
he yawned or stretched himself, Hugh Langmayde,
the priest in gray, lost naught of what he did; and at
last, still watching this gallant, he fell to open talk with
himself after this fashion:

"Soon shall you stretch those sturdy limbs, my boy,
And for your rapier find a brave employ.
I am too old, too feeble; — you alone
Shall do this sacred errand of our Lord,
Avenge his murdered saints, and from her throne
Cast down this Jezebel, of men abhorred.
I thought not, when I taught thy youth to know
One creed, one king, and questionless to go
Where church or king decreed, that you and I,
As if we were but one, like head and hand,
Should free this England which doth fettered lie,
And give to God another Christian land.

"What if my weapon fail me? Restless grown,
He asks now this, now that, would have me own
My purpose,— hath the waywardness of youth,—
Is wilful, petulant, or grave. In truth,
It shall mean little when he comes to learn
What splendid bribe an eager hand may earn,
And at my will he goes my way to win
God's gold or this world's guerdon. Is it sin

To shudder thinking death may be his lot?
My task were easier if he loved me not.
God's priest should die unloved; should have no fears,
Live without memories, and know not tears."

Herewith the young gallant, Philip Vernon by name,
calls out to a servant of the inn:

" Fetch me some ale, good fellow. Set it here —
Two brimming tankards. See 't is cool and clear.
— How fresh the air! I like this breezy shade
The better since by sunshine it is made.
Our Spanish saying aptly hits my mark:

        Soar with the hawk,
        Sing with the lark;
        Eyes for the sunlight,
        Lips for the dark.

St. James! I 'm weary of my unused self,
Left like a dull book on a dusty shelf.
I hate this corner life! Now, by the Cid!
I must be more discreet. I 'm sternly bid
To hide my name because my name may lead —
I know not why — to questions that exceed
Our skill to answer fitly. — Master Hugh,
Come taste with me our host's last autumn brew."

Hearing his call, the priest, smiling, sits down beside
the young man he had been gravely watching; and
taking of the ale, — but with a wry face, for in Spain

he had learned dislike of such honest English drink,—
he lays a hand on the lad's knee, and says to him:

"What troubles you, my Philip?"

PHILIP VERNON.   We have strayed
  Now here, now there, in England while you played
  A game, good Father, somewhat like the chess
  Our prior loved. You smile on me,— my guess
  Has hit the butt? Here moves a pawn, and there,
  Haply, a bishop. Then the queen —

HUGH LANGMAYDE.   Beware!
  You chatter lightly, call me "Father,"— try
  To lose the habit; that way dangers lie.
  One careless word, and rack and axe or rope
  Await us; and so dies the saintliest hope
  This misruled kingdom knows. To die were gain
  For me; and yet God's work, the church, our Spain,
  The king, our master, own me till this strife
  With evil ends. Be patient!

PHILIP VERNON.   Oh, this life
  Of masquerade, and lies, and daily fear
  Of what I know not, wearies me!

HUGH LANGMAYDE.   Not here
  The time or place for truant tongues. Speak low,
  Or, better, change the talk.

PHILIP VERNON.   Soon I must know.

The priest, emptying his tankard and pushing it from him, looks askance at his companion, and therewith says, as if to quiet his mind with other thought:

"Poor stuff is this beside our convent wine.
You need but squeeze the ripeness of the vine
To drain its reddest blood:—torment the grains
God meant for bread, and lo! you get for pains
This boorish drink."

And now is heard a quick rattle of horse-hoofs, and a score of gentles come down the road at speed. Some are armed, and more are clad in gay doublets, with plumes unmeet for riding—sign of haste, perchance. Red, blue, and purple, with glint of steel, flash through the yellow dust, aglow with the sun of noon, as the riders go by the inn. But three draw rein beneath the oaks; whereon this Philip Vernon leaps up, oversetting a flagon of good ale, and crying:

"Look, look, ye saints! That roan,
And that dark chestnut,—his who rode alone,—
Are worth a prince's ransom! See—they stay
To breathe their horses. He with plume of gray
Hath the best seat. Red Doublet's all untrussed:
He must have ridden hard; and, see,—the dust!
Why ride they thus?"

As he speaks the servants and landlord come hastily forth from the inn.

HUGH LANGMAYDE.   Hush! Out comes all the hive.
You shall know shortly.

RED DOUBLET.   Ho! are none alive?
The Armada 's off the Lizard. Look aright
That all your headland beacons blaze to-night!
These be Lord Howard's orders. Ho, there, quick!
Ale, ale,—three flagons!

GRAY PLUME.   Wine, wine! I am sick
With dusty thirst.

RED DOUBLET.   And I could drink a tun.

As they sit in the saddle, the fair maid of the inn
brings to each his flagon of ale.

ONE ARMED IN A CUIRASS. Keep me some kisses.

RED DOUBLET.   I shall ask but one.

MAID. Oh, my good lords, there shall not lack a prayer
From one poor wench that God your lives will spare.
Alas! alas! I 'm mightily afraid
Scarce will be left a man to kiss a maid!
This dreadful war!—

GRAY PLUME.   Now, by the gods! but *he*
Will truly have his hands full.—This for thee!
—The admiral rides hard, and we must sup
Aboard the ships.—Thanks for the stirrup-cup.

A hand on the bridle,
A cup of good sack;
Pray keep those lips idle
Until I come back.

RED DOUBLET.

Here 's a curse on Romish rats!
Here 's good luck to English cats!

Then he who wore a cuirass, as they ride away sings
lustily:

"'T is always pleasant weather
In the company of wine;
And the mile-stones run together,
And the roughest road is fine,
In the company of wine.
For no man owes a shilling,
And all the land is thine,
And every lip is willing
In the company of wine."

LANDLORD. God keep our England merry!

PHILIP VERNON. Who be they
Who ride so hotly at full noon of day?

LANDLORD. Howard of Effingham, Lord High Admiral,
A lover of the Pope, and yet withal
A sturdy gentle, English to the core,
And hates a Spaniard. What can one say more?

HUGH LANGMAYDE.   Where rides he now?

LANDLORD.   To Plymouth Port.   The coast
Is all astir.   The great Armada's host
Is come at last.   God help our little fleet! .

HUGH LANGMAYDE.   God help the right and England!

LANDLORD.   Aye.

PHILIP VERNON.   Retreat
Could scarce fly swifter than these gallants ride.
I would, good Father, I were at their side.

Hereon Hugh Langmayde and Philip together leave
the inn and highroad, and as they slowly climb a little
hill, and begin to enter into a wood of oak, the priest
makes this answer to the lad's vexation of spirit:

" Peace, boy!   Thy ways are in a nobler path.
They ride to death.   Already God's stern wrath
Is gathering for their ruin on the seas.
Come with me, Philip.   There among the trees
Talk will be safer.   Come,— the hour of fate
Is near at hand.   You shall no longer wait
To hear the tale I ofttimes promised you
When, the day's lessons done, at fall of dew
Above Grenada from the convent wall
We watched the paling gold of evening crawl
From peak to peak, while o'er the Vega's plain
The dusking shadows marched.   Thus, not in vain,

When all the lower world is dim and gray,
God sets the promise of another day
On those his church has taught to live above
Man's mist of passions,—aye, and earthly love."

THE CHASE

As they move through the wood the priest pauses at
last where from a hillside the more open forest com-
mands a broad view of green fields, the river with
hills beyond, and to left the distant sea.

PHILIP VERNON.   How still it is, how full of peace, how far
From the rude hurry and alarm of war!
See what an airy build the mountains show
When over them the broad-winged shadows go.
A land to love!

HUGH LANGMAYDE.   Aye, and a land to serve
With noble deeds that may indeed deserve
This splendid recompense. A land to win
Back from its damned covenant with sin.
Sit here, my son. Once this great fallen tree
Looked o'er the land, and could no equal see.
Lord of the forest, underneath its shade
The wanderer rested. Here both man and maid

2

Found shelter. High among its eaves
The birds sang hymns which God alone had taught,
Or nested peaceful in its spreading leaves,
Where sun and rain His mystic wonders wrought.

PHILIP VERNON. I see not clearly, Father,—

HUGH LANGMAYDE.   No, my son;
A nation wandered from the fold, undone,
Sunk in delusion, waits full many a year,—
Waits for God's hour to read that riddle clear.
Once, in this land, the Church spread broad and high
The mighty leafage of her destiny —
Why mince my meaning? Lo! a brutal king
Struck, and the splendid trunk lies moldering.

PHILIP VERNON. And still I see not wherefore—

HUGH LANGMAYDE.   Ah! The rest
Attends your hearing. Soon this land oppressed
Shall know deliverance. O'er yon waiting sea
Great Philip's viceroy comes. To you, to me,
God grants on land as sure a victory.
And now, my Philip, hear me to an end.
In happier times I shall be glad to mend
My broken story of your life. To-day
Accept a briefer tale. I have grown gray
Now many years, since through these woods I fled,
A hunted priest, this land where God seemed dead.

Pursuit was hot; my boat lay off the shore;
A bullet caught me as I plunged; a score
Flew over. Still this crippled leg, my lad,
Keeps me a memory not wholly sad;
For, as I bleeding strove, a boy's white face
Rose in a black wave's hollow. By God's grace
I clutched your hand, my son. The boat's crew caught
The pair of us, half drowned; and so God wrought
This great deliverance. I think the tide
Trapped you at play on yonder sands. I tried
To set you safe upon the coast. 'T was vain;
I could not do the thing I would. In Spain
The fevered life I scarce had hope to save
Came back as if new born, as if the grave
That was so near had taken half away
Your boyhood's recollections. Need I say
Love to my heart came easily? I yearned
To win the love my double help had earned.

PHILIP VERNON.

You have it in full measure. Now at last
I shall know all. Is this to end that past
Of doubts, and dreams, and fears? Before my eyes,
Lo! as you speak, faint memories arise.

HUGH LANGMAYDE. Trust them not wholly.

PHILIP VERNON. I 've a vision wild
Of ravening seas; and them beyond, a child,

I live again glad days. I seem indeed
Like one who, waking from a dream, has need
To piece it out with thinking. Who is he —
A stately gentleman, I strive to see,
And cannot clearly, though he smiles? Stay, stay!
Was that my father? As you love me, say!
Was it my father? Ah! so much is dim;
But that has substance. Let me go to him —
Yes, you and me together. I can hear
How he will thank you.

HUGH LANGMAYDE.   — Wherefore should I fear
To know at last if I have truly read
The soul I trained?

PHILIP VERNON.   Why hesitate? You dread
To speak some truth!

HUGH LANGMAYDE.   You do not ask to know
Your name and station?

PHILIP VERNON.   Let that matter go.
Where is my father?

HUGH LANGMAYDE.   Can I give the dead?

PHILIP VERNON. Dead! And how long ago?

HUGH LANGMAYDE.   Two years, 't is said.

PHILIP VERNON.
Dead! Two years dead! Know you the hour, the
day?

HUGH LANGMAYDE. I know them not.

PHILIP VERNON. And I may have been gay,
And laughed, or diced, the hour he passed away!

As he ceases, the priest, who has watched him
moodily, touches his arm as if in appeal, whereupon
the young man exclaims:

" Nay, do not speak. How very often here
He must have wandered, and when death drew near
Thought of this son in heaven! Some might fear
To cheat the living and the dead. Despair
Seems but a thing of earth. How could you dare
To cast its shadow on a world beyond!"

HUGH LANGMAYDE.
My more than child, ah, when this earthly bond
Of love is severed, surely God has power
To heal the sorrows of earth's little hour.

As if not hearing the priest, and with yet more of
anger, the younger man continues:

" My God! Those years of youth when I in Spain,
And he in England, took our ignorant pain
To God, and never knew what statecraft stole
Of nature's honest store! You took the whole —
All, all of love two lives had! By my soul,
I think that you must see forevermore
A gray-haired man who walks beside the shore,
And of the silent ocean asks his dead!"

HUGH LANGMAYDE. You wrong me, Philip.

PHILIP VERNON.   No, I should have fled —
  Oh, long ago — had I known all; but now
  'T is past the cure of word or deed. Ah, how —
  How could you hurt me thus?

HUGH LANGMAYDE.   I did God's will —
  His and the king's.

PHILIP VERNON.   The king's! Could he fulfil
  What home and father would have given?

HUGH LANGMAYDE.   My son,
  Pray you consider. Could I aught have done
  Against the king's command? I did not dare.
  What lack you else the gentle born should bear?
  Head, hand, and eye have had such anxious care
  As only Spain can give. What English peer
  Has court or camp trained better? Do you fear
  To cross a sword with any? Who, I ask,
  Can match you mounted? Mine the graver task
  To see you lack not learning. Pause, reflect;
  Not without prayer I acted. You suspect
  Some treason? — Philip, where you stand to-day
  The soil is yours. That castle old and gray,
  The river's sweep, hill, forest, town, and lake,
  In God's good time are yours, my son, to take.
  See where yon eagle o'er the mountain soars!

Scarce can he look beyond what land is yours.
Set foot in stirrup, draw your father's sword:
A thousand men will follow you, my lord!
Low at your word will bow that tavern churl,
And I shall bid you welcome, my Lord Earl!

PHILIP VERNON.

    Earl! Lord! These manors mine? You could
      not jest.

HUGH LANGMAYDE.

    Not I, my lord; you match with England's best.
    The proofs that give you these the Church will
      guard
    Till one proud day of triumph and reward.

PHILIP VERNON.

    'T is a strange tale, and sad as it is strange.
    I would a braver love had bid you change
    Those home-reft years I have forever lost.
    You should have counted well the cruel cost,
    And saved my life this pain. Oh, bitter day!
    Vexed with a convent life, made next to play
    A page's part, or squire's, left to say
    I knew not who I was, or high or base,
    Until, worn out, I smote a snarling face
    That mocked my birth as knowing some disgrace;
    For text of thought he got a rapier thrust.
    Alas! I gave you all my boyhood's trust,
    And thus you used it!

HUGH LANGMAYDE.   Philip, that same breath
  With which you question me, I gave; the death
  From which I saved you set a silent grave
  Between the lost life and the life I gave.
  You have a father. Have I seemed to be
  Less than a father?

PHILIP VERNON.   None were that to me.
  I have been hurt enough: 't were well to spare
  These convent subtleties. In England fair
  I tread where men are free, breathe lighter air.
  Much have I learned no Spanish cloister taught,
  More have I heard that Spain had never thought.

HUGH LANGMAYDE.
  Ill have you heard. Not all my tale is told.
  Let but the Church her lifting hand withhold,
  And you are lost! Be her true son, be bold,
  And these broad lands are yours to win when she
  Who rules this kingdom dies. For you, for me,
  The path lies straight. But yestermorn in prayer
  I asked of God a sign, and found it where
  At close of eve I sat and saw the sun
  Set in a sea of blood ere day was done —
  A cloud-born cross above. Oh, dark shall be
  The Church's reckoning when yon loathing sea
  Its unrepentant dead spits on the shore,
  And the long torment of the galley's oar
  Shall chain the souls that live! What seek you
      more?

PHILIP VERNON.

> What more indeed! I went your way, not mine,
> Knew but one prince, sought never to divine
> Your reasons, nor the policy of state
> That without explanation ruled my fate.
> Answer my manhood outright! Be more true
> To one who loves you! Give me all love's due.
> What keeps us here? I will not be denied.
> An English noble! Wherefore should I bide
> Upon your will my father's lands to claim
> While pope and king play out a doubtful game?

HUGH LANGMAYDE.

> You ask untimely. Shall the arrow know
> The stern commission of the bended bow?
> In God's good time —

PHILIP VERNON.   The hour that is, is good;

> No other answers. Ah, I think you should
> Have known me better. Speak! By good St. James,
> I 'm very weary of these priestly games!
> I take it that, as well as one can see
> Through this dim, wordy haze of mystery,
> I rest mere Philip Vernon until death
> Strikes with your hand, or mine, Elizabeth.
> Is that your meaning, Father? If 't is so,
> We part to-day. Oh, I must clearly know
> What the cowl's caution hid from me. Be frank,
> As you were wont. Give me new cause to thank
> The man within the priest.

3

HUGH LANGMAYDE.   Go, if you will.
    If God and king, my danger, and these years
    Of love lack force to teach you duty still,
    Go! Leave me here to peril and to tears.

PHILIP VERNON.
    Love is not bondage; and, for that harsh king,
    I owe him hate alone.— Oh, do not wring
    My heart with more of grief! Tell me the tale
    Of who and what I am.— There cannot fail
    To be some light, some guidance, some poor path
    Out of this mystery!

HUGH LANGMAYDE.   The Lord's just wrath
    Will punish this revolt.

PHILIP VERNON.   I do not change
    As shifts the weathervane! Hold you it strange
    I should learn English ways?— But yesterday
    I fell to talking with a gallant gay—
    Upon my soul, a rare, sweet gentle he,
    Hidalgo born, a flower of chivalry,
    Simple and courteous, melancholic now,
    And now as merry as a May-day queen,
    With chat of court and camp and state, a brow,
    Just helmet-dinted, o'er an eye serene
    That made swift capture of my inward thought
    Before a word my tardy tongue had wrought.

Sir Philip Sidney he! We talked full long
Of Spain and England, of what cruel wrong
My jailor Philip did, and soon we passed
To speak of Spain's Armada. "Now," at last,
"Thank God for war!" he cried. "The die is cast!
And you, a gentleman, young sir,"— to me,—
"Sit in a tavern sad, while history
Is in the mighty making." Then he quaffed
A cup of wine. "Is it a woman?"—laughed
Because, shame-flushed, I, angry, answered not.
"Pardon," he added. "Cast the iron lot
Of war, and take with us the splendid chance.
God and the queen, a sword, a horse, a lance!
Your name, fair sir?" I could but hang my head.
What could I answer? "I have none," I said.
— You bade me hide it, you were well .obeyed.
He touched my shoulder kindly: "Many a man
Has found a proud name where the red blood ran.
Aimless and nameless? Get you aim and name
Where two great nations play war's royal game.
Come with me on the morrow."

HUGH LANGMAYDE.   And you cried,
    Vade Sathanas!

PHILIP VERNON.   Nay, I naught replied,
    Or scarce a word. By Heaven, I had been right
    To follow loyally that gallant knight
    Where England calls her sons!

HUGH LANGMAYDE.   What! must I fail
For this boy folly?—You shall hear the tale,—
Aye, all of it a tender heart withheld
To give more gently in the happier hour
God's victory will bring. Ah, then dispelled
Were half its anguish!

PHILIP VERNON.   Speak! I have the power
To bear life's very worst.

HUGH LANGMAYDE.   Is this the lad
I saved from death? Defiant, reckless, mad,
You ask you know not what.

PHILIP VERNON.   But I will know,
And on the minute, or by Heaven! I go
To claim what rights are mine.

HUGH LANGMAYDE.   You court the fate
That bides for him who does not know to wait
On God's maturing hour. Alas, poor fool!
Art nameless? Yes! This, on my oath to rule
A froward nature, by the rood I swear!
Didst hear?—the rood! Thou art a bastard born!
Art fitly answered? Didst thou think to dare
To cross my purpose,—thou, a child of scorn!

PHILIP VERNON.
What fool's device is this? A little while
I was my lord, am now a bastard vile.

Another man this pleasant tale should rue
All the brief life I 'd leave him.

HUGH LANGMAYDE.   Still, 't is true.

PHILIP VERNON.   By Heaven, thou liest!

HUGH LANGMAYDE.   Have I ever lied?

PHILIP VERNON.   God knows, not I.

HUGH LANGMAYDE.   I should have naught replied.
A priest, and lie! It seems a challenge cheap.
Tears!—that is wiser. Oh, I did but keep
My better tidings back. Alas, no friend
Could hide this ill news long, or know to mend
A wrong of birth; but when, in God's good time,
Your arm has freed a land, and yonder chime
Rings in our king, rings out this fated queen,
Then she who owns this broad domain has seen
Her last of greatness.

PHILIP VERNON.   Who?

HUGH LANGMAYDE.   Your cousin,—she,
Your father's heir, your steward now till we
Win Philip's battle, and his potent hand
Strikes from your shield the bastard's shameful band,
Gives all I promised, honor, wealth, and place,—
All that men covet in this earthly race.
Go! I have done. Think on it for the week
We linger here. Be prudent, slow to speak,

Watchful and wise. God's hand is on the helm,
And I, the church, the king, this woeful realm
Will need your help.

PHILIP VERNON.   I would that I could doubt
    One who has never lied. I stand without
    The pale of honor and the hopes of men,
    A nameless creature, bred to turn again
    And rend the race that gave me, with this stain,
    Intrepid honor, proud desires,— in fine,
    The manly virtues of a noble line.
    Poor useless jewels! all in vain their worth.
    I had been happier made of meaner earth.

HUGH LANGMAYDE.
    Nay, nay; but that 's not so. Land, title, place,
    Are yours to gain when, by God's helping grace,
    That Spanish dagger at your side strikes quick.
    Oh, I can see,— can *see* this heretic
    Roll bloody in the dust, and hear the land
    Ring joy from spire to spire!

PHILIP VERNON.   I understand
    At last too well. No more for me the prayer
    To be delivered from temptation's snare.

HUGH LANGMAYDE. Sad words, my son!

PHILIP VERNON.   Yet heed them well: they say
    The malice of dishonor. If I prey
    Like maggots on the carcass whose decay

Begot my baseness, who shall blame the banned?
What wouldst thou of me? Is it head or hand?

HUGH LANGMAYDE.

How beautiful the evening is! Behold
The dim, green meadows take the dewy gold,
While in the hollows little pools of mist
Are gathering slowly where the cattle list
The milky summons of the twilight horn.
Look! 'T is your heritage! Some men are born
Ignobly great; some in one matchless hour
Scale at a bound the heights of human power.

PHILIP VERNON.

A bastard lord! Not I! Awhile ago
You took from life its beauty and its glow.
How could you mock my fancies with a tale
Such as my boyhood dreamed, and let it fail
In such a slough of shame? Love, honor, hope —
You took them all, and offer now a rope.
'T is kind! I was a man, and you have made
A fiend of whom you well might be afraid
If you had lied.— You could not.— Take me! Use
My strength, my will, my hate, as you may choose.

HUGH LANGMAYDE.   There 's time to think.

PHILIP VERNON.   Not I ! What next?

HUGH LANGMAYDE.   Wilt swear?

PHILIP VERNON.
    Aye, for an oath is only empty air.
    Once 't was a thing to spend a life for. I
    Am but a hireling now mere gold may buy,
    Or any Judas coin.

As Philip speaks he makes a move as if to go, but of
a sudden returning, looks the priest steadily in the
face, and with a troubled countenance says to him:

            " One word to close
An hour the damned might pity. I suppose —
— There was a mother—
             — Well ? "

HUGH LANGMAYDE.   Long, long ago
    Your mother died.

PHILIP VERNON.   'T is all I care to know.
    Loved, sinned, and died! May God's sweet pity rest
    Upon the shameless woman from whose breast
    I drew the milk of sorrows!

HUGH LANGMAYDE.   Sleep and prayer
    Will bring you peace, yet leave you power to dare
    A deed with which the world shall ring. Good
        night.
    In three days I return again. To right
    Your pathway lies toward the inn. Invite
    No comment. Guard yourself. Good night.

As the priest moves away Philip Vernon replies
   tardily:

                                        "Good night.
What night is good to me? Alas, what day?"

THE GARDEN

WALKING slowly away, Philip Vernon takes his sad-
ness deeper into the woods, and wandering far, comes
at last to a great garden wall. There he stays awhile,
until sweet odors, rising, seem to call him; and with
no more thought of what may lie beyond, he leaps the
wall, and stands amid the flowers, waist-deep in holly-
hock and golden-plume.

"I wonder somewhat was my life then· gay
When here I chased the butterflies, and trod
These garden lanes, or rolled upon the sod
A thoughtless boy? I 'll take, for memory's sake,
One rose of home."

Hither into the garden at this moment comes Lord
Francis Grey, in red velvet, with a face aflame to
match. Seeing this gallant across a hedge of sweet-

4

peas, he slips the collar of his humor and sets it on to
bite in this wise:

> "Ho! Who are you who break
> These castle bounds at will? Ho there! Take heed!
> Didst hear me?"

PHILIP VERNON. Yes. Your words, I think, exceed
The owner's power to back his tongue at need.

LORD GREY.
My cousin is the chancellor's ward; none dare
Avenge an insult here.

PHILIP VERNON. Then wiser 't were
To keep the tongue in ward. You question one
That hath lost touch of fear beneath the sun.
The chancellor? What care I? Your cousin?
Mine?
Now, why not mine? Suppose, to cap the jest,
We fight for cousinship: who wins is best.
And is she fair, this woman? Doth her talk,
Like thine, lack breeding? This smooth garden
walk
Is broad enough to serve us. Draw, on guard!
And let my rapier teach your tongue such ward
As hasty manners lack.

LORD GREY. Have then your will!
Or mad or foolish, you 're a man to kill!
Yet to cross blades with one unknown or base —

PHILIP VERNON.

    Base! By my soul! Were you his very Grace,
This same lord chancellor, his mighty face
Should know my glove!

Lord Grey, having already drawn his sword, advances
and lunges smartly at Philip, at the same time crying
out:
"By Heaven, you are dead!"

PHILIP VERNON.

    A thing, observe, less easily done than said.
A step more near, a trifle yet more quick,
And you had boasted shrewdly. Oh, the trick
Is stale. In Spain we lunge this wise, and then
A thrust in tierce — Well parried! — Good, again!
I take it firmly close to hilt; the wrist
Well up; then deftly, with this cunning twist,
Give point. Your sword-arm? By the Cid, 't is sad!
That stops the sport.

LORD GREY.   'T is not so very bad
    But that a day will cure it.

At this he sees men break through the shrubbery and
come running toward them, whereon he says to Philip:

                  "Get you gone!
There, by the terrace, and across the lawn.

PHILIP VERNON. And wherefore?

LORD GREY. Hasten, leap the brook and fly!

As Philip stands with no mind to escape, the steward
and many servants gather around them.

STEWARD.
What means this brawl? My lady asks, not I.

LORD GREY.
'T is but a. trifle. Come with me. The blame
I shall stand father to. This way. The dame?—

STEWARD. Is in the eastern gallery.

LORD GREY. Best it were
You tarry here awhile. My cousin fair
Has many humors: which shall be our share
No man has skill to tell. Her No, or Yes,
A hundred years' experience could not guess.

With these words Lord Grey leaves Philip Vernon
at the entrance of the castle, where, with sudden in-
terest in his face, he looks about him, and at last
says:

"How most familiar 't is! There the great hall,
The windowed gallery, and on the wall
The gray stone dial. There the poplars tall.
Now, as I live, the willows and the brook!
And there my father sat the while I took

His great horse o'er it,—much I feared the leap.
How memory wakens as if from a sleep !
The stair! Sir Lancelot's armor! That brave lance
Lord Arthur carried to the wars in France.
One night I touched it—on the floor it crashed,
And the fierce strife of Crécy round me clashed
With din of spear and steed, and shock and blow,
And clang of knights that set my heart aglow."

A Servant.
    My lady bids me say for her, Sir Knight,
    She waits you in the gallery. Here, to right.

    Philip Vernon enters the picture-gallery, and sees at
    the far end Elizabeth Vernon speaking with Lord
    Grey.

Lord Grey.   The errant knight waits yonder.

Elizabeth Vernon.   Let him wait;
    'T is a man's business. Now, I pray you, state
    What means this quarrel?

Lord Grey.   Ask of yonder man.

. Elizabeth Vernon.
    Man! Why not gentle, cousin? Never ran
    Mean blood in one like him, who there, at ease,
    In courteous silence stands. Now, an you please,
    What more, my lord?

LORD GREY.   I found the man you see
    A-picking roses 'neath your balcony.

ELIZABETH VERNON.
    Why, this should hang him on the nearest tree!
    And my blunt cousin picked, for company,
    A quarrel. That is easier than a rose.
    He found a thorn, as rather plainly shows
    That crimsoned sleeve.

LORD GREY.   Now look you, Cousin Bess,
    Your jest is but ill-timed. Let me confess
    I made this quarrel when, my heart aflame,
    You left me stinging with your words. The blame
    Is yours, fair cousin. Shafts in anger sent
    May find mad errands ere their force be spent.

ELIZABETH VERNON. Now, by our Lady!

LORD GREY.   Nay, but hear me still;
    And let your servants know at least your will
    That yonder venturer go on his way,
    And no such words escape as haply may
    Breed risks for me.

ELIZABETH VERNON.   I shall consider first
    When I have questioned him, nor shall the worst
    Be worse, my lord, than what has chanced. You
        claim
    Such license here as men may justly blame.

Best choose a fitter place, a feebler prey,
To hawk at with your anger.

At this Lord Grey, turning to one side, mutters to
himself as he glances down the hall at Philip:

                              " He shall pay
His debt and yours, my lady. Those who court
Tongue-tilts with wounded creatures, find the sport
A doubtful venture. ' By the Cid,' he swore;
Mocked me with Spanish sword-play. Ah! my score
Is easily settled."

ELIZABETH VERNON.   You are silent, sir?

LORD GREY.
I school my hurt heart to soft words, for her
Whose lightest word my very blood can stir;
And if in aught I have exceeded, rest
Assured I meant it not. Were it not best
I set this errant knight without your gate?

ELIZABETH VERNON.
No. I would speak with him. Pray do not wait:
My temper 's of the shortest. On your way
Send me the gentleman; and, cousin, stay!—
I 'll have no gossip.

Lord Grey, sullenly walking down the hall, pauses
beside Philip Vernon:

"We shall meet again!
My lady waits. And for those tricks of Spain
I shall be readier. Good day."

PHILIP VERNON.   'T is plain
I was imprudent.

As he moves up the hall toward Elizabeth Vernon,
she watches him, speaking to herself the while:

"Where saw I those eyes,
Large, gray, and watchful? Some elate surprise
Is in their gaze.—

I pray you pardon us
This most uncourteous hour. It is not thus
We welcome unknown comers. I have heard
You would be nameless: so is every bird
That wings my garden. And 't is said you stole
A rose or two. If that be all,—the whole
Of this last hour's sin,— I hold you shriven;
Aye, and that lesson to a fool forgiven."

PHILIP VERNON. I thank you, madam.

ELIZABETH VERNON.   Am I, sir, a book,
That you would read me with that eager look?

PHILIP VERNON.
Oft have I read you. I am wont to share
My idle hours with you.

ELIZABETH VERNON.   Indeed, sir?

PHILIP VERNON.   Where
   The chase o'erhangs your garden, oft I sit
And read you page by page, nor want I wit
To comment on your sweetness.

ELIZABETH VERNON.   You are bold
   Past nurtured manners.

PHILIP VERNON.   Pardon me, I told
   But half my heart says.

ELIZABETH VERNON.   Sir, an hour ago
   We were but strangers.

PHILIP VERNON.   Ere the sand shall flow
   Another hour, we shall be strange once more,
And ever strange.

ELIZABETH VERNON. Is this some Quixote, mad,
   That loved and lost, and cannot live it o'er?
— By all the saints, I think it very sad
To see good wits astray.

PHILIP VERNON.   Are mine astray?
   It seems they wandered wisely. Let them say
What saner wits would shun. The shyest maid
That ever loved, and, loving, grew afraid,
Would braver be to set her love in words.
Mine hath uncertain wings, like new-born birds,
And may not think on heaven. Forgive, forget!
Think me a lover wild, of brain once met
   5

In some freaked tale of eld,— a prince of fay
That came, and loved, and lost, and rode away.

ELIZABETH VERNON.   That 's a wild riddle.

PHILIP VERNON.   Time owns not the hour
Shall give some buds the answer of a flower.
You have been very gentle with a man
Who dare not name himself, who never can
Do more than thank your kindness.   I am one
Accursed and nameless till my days be done.
How you have helped me you may never know,
Nor what you saved us both.   I came your foe;
More than your friend I leave.   Just Heaven knows
How sad my life has been.   Let this one rose
I took for—well, no matter—let me guard
This rose for memory.   It will make less hard
The strife of days to come.

ELIZABETH VERNON.   You speak like one
By some strange cruelty of fate undone.
Be plain.

PHILIP VERNON.   I may not further.

ELIZABETH VERNON.   Then take hence
A woman's prayer for peace.   There 's no offense
In honest words, and none did ever speak
Words that more sadly touched me.   I am weak
Where women should be.   There 's no need to say
'T is but mere weakness.   Must you, then, away?

PHILIP VERNON.

    I dare not — must not — linger. Here to stay
Were to tempt folly. Ah, you may divine
All that my honor bids my heart resign.
So fades another dream. Alack! alack!
Dreams are but dreams,— we may not dream them
    back.
Take you an exile's thanks. This gracious hour
Shall live remembered.

As he walks away, Elizabeth Vernon whispers to
herself:

               "Still those eyes have power
To tease dull memory with some strange surmise,
And trouble expectation."

Philip, walking down the gallery and seeing the por-
traits on the walls, stops abruptly; whereupon Elizabeth Vernon adds:

              "What surprise
So moves this stranger?"

PHILIP VERNON.   There 's the Lady Blanche,
That held the castle; there the baron stanch,
Who rode to battle laughing. Am I heir,
Through him, of that mad merriment I share
When swords are out and death is in the air?
My father's face! So gracious too!— by Heaven!
Now I can say, "Be all thy sin forgiven!"

And thank the gentle hand that swept away
The desperate counsels of a darker day.

For a moment he stands before the portrait, and then
goes slowly down the gallery, and leaves the castle.

THE CHASE

Two days later, in the afternoon of the summer day,
Philip Vernon walks here and there in the great forest, and at last, leaning against a tree, speaks thus to
himself:

"How wearily the hours go by! This chase
I haunt, as haunts a bird the lonely place
That holds her pillaged nest."

Seeing him of a sudden, Elizabeth Vernon comes
timidly through the thickets.

ELIZABETH VERNON.　　　　　　　　I thought, Sir Knight,
You had been far from this. I would quick flight
Had set you miles away. I more than fear
My cousin's treachery. What keeps you here
Is much in question, and in days of war
The questioned man is lost. You should be far
From this to-morrow.

PHILIP VERNON. Not while dangers grow
So thick about one frail old man.

ELIZABETH VERNON. I know
Of you, of him, no more than what I hear
From one who hates you, yet enough to fear
For you such peril as may cost too dear
Some woman heart at home.

PHILIP VERNON. Ah, there are none
Will weep for me. Of all that live not one.
As alien ships that only meet to part,
Thy life and mine have crossed on stormy seas.
Learn to forget. 'T is a most wholesome art.

ELIZABETH VERNON.
An art that women practise with less ease
Than men.

PHILIP VERNON.
There 's time to learn it, for no more
Shall we two meet.

ELIZABETH VERNON. No more!

PHILIP VERNON. Dear heart, no more.
I said forget. How could I say forget?
No, rather let some shadow of regret
Still haunt thy better fortunes in glad hours
When Spring is come again, and with her flowers

Arise frail memories and thoughts long dumb,
That are the wildings of the mind, and come
With Nature's yearning season.

ELIZABETH VERNON.   Hush! I heard
Steps in the wood.

PHILIP VERNON.   No, not a leaf has stirred.

ELIZABETH VERNON.
I am grown fearful. If you would but go
While the near hour is gracious —

PHILIP VERNON.   No; ah, no!
Not for the bribe of love.

ELIZABETH VERNON.   If, sir, you loved,
My prayer were quickly answered. You 'd be moved,
And fly.

PHILIP VERNON. You will not ask it. Those proud eyes
Would turn with scorn from him whose honor dies.
Men call me traitor: but, my lady fair,
That died in me when all of my despair
I cast before your feet. What mercy lies
In the sweet equity of honest eyes
I gladly trust.

ELIZABETH VERNON. Thank Heaven, I know not, sir,
What sad temptation may have bid you err.
I would not—will not—know. Do you forget
I suffer while you linger here?

PHILIP VERNON.   And yet
   I cannot go. I would we had not met,
   Or God had given to me a kinder fate,
   A less uncertain birth, a nobler state.

ELIZABETH VERNON.
   Uncertain, said you?

PHILIP VERNON.   Yes, I said it,—yes.
   For that time has no comfort, no redress,
   And you are worlds away. But here, alone,
   Once let me speak. The falcon love has flown
   Where the proud instinct of his haughty wings
   Takes love that soars. Beneath it earth's mean
      things
   Grow half unreal, and the morning rings
   With new-born light his world of wish and will.
   I love you — love you. Be it well or ill,
   Still shall I love you. None may ever doubt
   Hope's dying words. Alas! my treason 's out.
   Oh, traitor heart!

Elizabeth Vernon looks at Philip, and of a sudden
seating herself upon a fallen tree, covers her face with
her hands, and is silent for a moment.

PHILIP VERNON.   You will not speak?

ELIZABETH VERNON.   Wait, wait!
   — My God, I love him!—Sir, as sad a fate

As yours will make my life and land the prize
Of some debt-burdened noble. It were wise
We part at once.

PHILIP VERNON.   At once!

ELIZABETH VERNON.   Be merciful!
Go while my blinded sight with tears is dull.
You have been cruel. Ah, I cannot see
For tears of pity both for you and me.

PHILIP VERNON.
And have I wounded you, my gentle dove?
That were most sad of all to hurt with love.
I have done wrong—

ELIZABETH VERNON.
                    Yes—no! Would you were spared
This most unhappy fortune!

As she ceases, Lord Grey comes abruptly into the
open space, and cries out:
                    " Neatly snared!
'T is well I chanced to come. And have you dared,
A maid, a Vernon, thus to blot our fame,
My mother's lineage? Go! Go, take your shame
Where shame is common. Off with you! Fie! fie!
Have you no blushes? For this masking spy,
Who lured you hither—"

PHILIP VERNON.   By my soul, you die!

They draw their swords as Hugh Langmayde, in haste coming through the wood, steps between them.

PHILIP VERNON.   Out of my path!

HUGH LANGMAYDE.

No! no!   In God's name, peace! The church forbids you.

Lord Grey falls back, sheathes his sword, and says:

"Easy 't is to cease
When finer nets are spread.   A priest, indeed!
And thus disguised.   In truth, it seems decreed
My double debt shall wait.— You, madam, need
No further words from me.   Begone with speed!"

ELIZABETH VERNON.   Oh, for one hour to be a man!

LORD GREY.   True, true!
That had been better.   There were less to rue.

PHILIP VERNON.

I shall be surely man enough for two;
And you, whose tongue is quicker than your blade,
Shall lack no lesson.

Lord Grey stands smiling, while Hugh Langmayde seizes Philip by the arm, and, drawing him away, says to him:

"Why have you delayed?
I waited long.   'T is like we are betrayed.
6

Lose not a minute; and if fall of night
Find me not with you at the ford, take flight:
I shall be dead. Now God protect the right!

Philip cries to Elizabeth Vernon as he follows the priest:

"I may not wait. Heaven keep you!"

Then, turning to Lord Grey, says haughtily, and with a bow:

"We shall meet."

LORD GREY.

Yes, where the gallows makes revenge complete.

With these words he walks swiftly away, while the priest and Philip hurry through the wood in the opposite direction, leaving Elizabeth Vernon, who for a time stands still in the deepening shadows, and looks along the path where her lover has gone.

THE FORD

AFTER dusk Philip Vernon, having waited long at the appointed ford, begins to walk to and fro uneasily, and says:

"How long he tarries! I have that to say
Will sorely hurt him; and yet, chance what may,
This treason ends. Who's there?

HUGH LANGMAYDE.   Come! We are gone,
Lost men, I fear.   The wood, the wood!   Ere dawn
We must be far from this.   One feeble fool
Upon the rack betrayed us.   Oh, that school
Makes ready scholars!   Death is close at hand.

As they leave the shore, the sound of men-at-arms
comes from above and below, and always nearing
them.

"All ways are closed.   O sad, unhappy land,
That was so near deliverance!   Here, my son,
Take this, and go."

The priest, fainting and in haste, gives to Philip a
packet.
                         "My earthly course is run."
PHILIP VERNON.
I will not leave you.   Quick!   The garden gate
I saw wide open.   Come!

The old man, helped, hurries through the chase.
As they cross an open space near the garden, the
moon comes out, and from a thicket the flash of
steel is seen, and the red blaze of half a dozen mus-
quetoons.   The priest stumbles, and groans; men
run forth, and, falling on Philip and his companion,
stab the priest, who falls within the arched and open
gateway of the garden of the castle, crying:

                         "Too late, too late!
Curse on the heretic!   Fly, Philip!"

PHILIP VERNON.   No!
    Not I, by Heaven!

And, standing within the gateway, he cries fiercely
as he fights:
                    "This for your coward blow,
You this for vengeance, and you this, and go
To hell that spawned you!"

As with cries and shouts the men fall back, there is
a brief pause, while Lord Grey comes forward, sword
in hand.

PHILIP VERNON.   Have a care, my lord!
    The place is somewhat narrow, and the sward
Gives but ill footing. Neither can I spare
To teach you tricks of fence to-day. Beware!
Habet! You have it. Yes, this under thrust
Is deadly dangerous. Never put your trust
In that weak parry — traitor! coward! take
This for my love! this for that old man's sake!

As Lord Grey staggers and falls, he cries to those
about him:

"In on him! seize him! Quick, the gate, the wall!"

Philip again attacks the men who are nearest, and
as they give way, retreating, he shuts the gate. Then,
kneeling, he lifts the priest's head, and exclaims:

"Ye saints, he 's dead! Now let what may befall;
No worse can come to me."

As Philip bends over the priest, he hears him groan and mutter:

> "Strike sure! You swore —
Kill, kill the heretic!"

PHILIP VERNON.   Alas!

HUGH LANGMAYDE.   There 's more,—
Christ, for a minute's life to speak! I said
Of her,— your mother,— something —

But even as the words are on his lips the priest's head drops, and he dies.

PHILIP VERNON.   He is dead!
God pity me, I loved him. Wrong or right,
I loved him well. Christ rest his soul to-night.

As he rises he hears voices and shots, and, instantly turning, flies through the shrubbery until, bewildered, he comes upon a doorway in the side wall of the castle, and, in the darkness stumbling in haste upon a narrow stairway, opens a door cautiously, and enters the chapel of the castle.

"Ye saints be praised! for I am well-nigh spent,
And here 's a little respite, Heaven sent."

Breathing fast and hard, the lad sinks exhausted on the chancel step.

"The only friend I had this evening died;
I would to God that I were by his side!

But the mere brute in us will show his teeth:
I fought as if all life were glad.—Beneath
This cross a child I knelt."

Of a sudden he leaps up at sight of one coming
through the darkness.

"Speak, or you die!"

ELIZABETH VERNON.
Mother of mercy! It is I! 't is I!
I thought you slain.

PHILIP VERNON.   I have one friend the less.
They 've killed my only father; none may guess
My utter loneliness.

ELIZABETH VERNON.   I hear men's feet.
Get you behind the altar.

PHILIP VERNON.   Kiss me, sweet;
That will make death seem easy.

ELIZABETH VERNON.   Go, make haste!

He obeys, and Elizabeth Vernon falls on her knees
before the crucifix.

ELIZABETH VERNON.
Oh, Mary Mother, pitiful and chaste!
Save! save him!

Here comes in hot haste the steward, with men-at-arms
and the Queen's officers.

STEWARD.   Peace! She prays!

The Lady Elizabeth rising, he says, as he comes
forward:

> "We seek in vain
The dead man's traitor comrade."

ELIZABETH VERNON.   Well, 't is plain
He hides not here. Search you the river-banks;
The hills beyond the chase. He shall have thanks
Who finds this Spanish ruffler. Go! make haste!
These ducats for his capture. See you waste
No time about the castle. Shall it hap
This Spanish fox would seek so plain a trap?

Upon this the steward and men leave the chapel, and
as the noise fades away Philip Vernon comes forward.

PHILIP VERNON. Right bravely done!

ELIZABETH VERNON.   God guard you!

At this Philip Vernon gives her that packet the priest
had given him, and, much troubled, says:

> "Here is this
Sits heavy on my conscience. Ere I miss
Thy dear face, take it; for I have no mind
To carry treason. Should you chance to find
Aught that may ruin men, I pray of you
Destroy it; burn it."

ELIZABETH VERNON.   Why not wait to view
What costs a minute? You have that to spare.
This altar lamp suffices. Rest you there.
Some one might enter on us unaware.

As she opens the packet and reads therein a great
surprise possesses her.

"This holds no treason; none! Where got you
    these?
The Vernon arms?—a locket?—mysteries
That much concern me."

PHILIP VERNON.   Answer I have none.
The good priest gave me these ere life was done.
I thought them dangerous.

ELIZABETH VERNON.   Letters out of Spain!
The king's grave attestation. Still in vain
I tax my cunning. Who are you that brought
This tale of wonder?

PHILIP VERNON.   Madam, I was taught
To call myself plain Philip Vernon. I
Was that in Spain.

ELIZABETH VERNON.   You Philip Vernon! Try
To tell me more. Is it indeed of you
What I find written here? Is—is it true?

PHILIP VERNON.
How can I know? The Jesuit, flying, found
A tired boy-swimmer floating as if drowned,
And kept him all these years in Spain.

ELIZABETH VERNON.   Think. Strive
Some memory of childhood to revive.

PHILIP VERNON.

　　Ah, but what matters it to me? They bring
　　No happy fortune. What am I? A thing
　　The sea refused to bury, which that priest
　　Caught for mere pity ere it died — the least,
　　Aye, least of men am I. A waif forlorn.
　　Only in name a Vernon. I have borne
　　That old man's silence long, till he of late
　　Cursed me with knowledge of my bastard fate,
　　To use my anguish in a desperate game —
　　For what cared I, the unreckoned child of shame?

ELIZABETH VERNON.

　　A bastard! bastard! No, my lord; the pride
　　Of twenty earls is in your veins. He lied
　　Who told you that. Look! look! these papers! See!
　　I am the heir no longer; you are he.

Philip staggers back against a marble effigy of a
boy on a tomb just behind him, and cries out:

　　"Christ help me! How I loved him! Yet he swore—
　　Swore by the rood! A priest! The rood! No more!
　　It cannot be."

ELIZABETH VERNON. It is. If less the gloom,
　　You might have seen, my lord, your very tomb
　　Behind you there. And fully on the scroll
　　How, Philip Vernon drowned, "his precious soul

　7

Is with the saints." Oh, I could laugh were death
Less neighbored to my mirth. Also it saith,
"A youth of parts; well loved," that 's very truth;
"Witty and virtuous, also learned" — forsooth,
I think I must have loved you in your youth,
And ever since, my Philip. What to do
I know not. Yes! let your sword counsel you.
Seek my Lord Howard, the High Admiral;
Tell him this story boldly. Aye, tell all —
All this strange story. Let what may befall,
You cannot lose my love. Go, go, my lord;
Only to England could my soul afford
This new-born hope. Go now; the Spanish fleet
Is on the seas. Go, Philip. When you meet
Your boyhood's jailers, strike for brave Queen Bess!
And for this Bess that is thy queen no less.
Go! I shall love you as no mortal man
Was ever loved of maid since love began.

PHILIP VERNON.

My God, I thank thee for this hour of grace.

As he speaks he kneels, and sets her hand to his
lips, and then looking up, says:

"Hope, honor, home, a land to serve, a face
Dear as the summer sun to prisoned men,
Life, trust, and love, I have them all again.

Love! By my soul, I would I knew a word
Unsoiled by this world's commerce — never heard,
Save by some ardent angel, that should say
My more than earthly love."

ELIZABETH VERNON.   Oh, haste away!
Let love teach haste. This for the stirrup-cup!
And now, God speed you! All the country 's up;
The highway 's watched; I think none guard the
    shore:
That way is safest. Here, this further door
Leads to the strand. Go, set those wits to see
What rose of honor you can pluck for me.

They go out of the chapel, and descend to the bank
of the river.

PHILIP VERNON.
Good night! Sweet night, that marries hope to love.

ELIZABETH VERNON.
Good night. God keep you, and all saints above!

She stands and watches him as his boat goes down
the river.

ELIZABETH VERNON.
Oh, I could cry, could laugh; and if I knew
A saint of laughter, I would pray that you
Do keep me merry for good cause. Alack,
Being but a maid, I would I had you back.

THE GARDEN

VERNON CASTLE OF A MORNING IN AUGUST, 1588

ELIZABETH VERNON walks amidst the flowers, an open
letter in her hand.

"Oh, the sweet morning and the sweeter news
That make me doubly glad! Ah, who would lose
The hours of grief that won this leave to smile
Through one long careless day of joy, the while
I wait a larger joy! Our smiles and tears
Have many meanings. I could weep to-day
For very joy; and yesterday my fears
Fetched me strange laughter, though my life seemed
    gray
With age of longing. Oh, be glad with me,
Ye English roses! See, the morning sun
Asks for the lifted face of prayer. The sea,
God's sea, laughs with us; we have won — have won!"

Thus speaking, Elizabeth Vernon walks to and fro
among the flowers, and sometimes pauses to shadow
her eyes with her hand, that she may look across
the river all a-glitter with the sun. But at last she
kneels on the sod, and, laughing, cries:

"I must kiss some one, something. You, red rose,
Will never whisper it if I suppose

You are my Philip. Kiss me, kiss me quick!
These be the lips I love. I 'll shut my eyes
So not to know it is not he. I 'm sick
For kisses. Ah, but when he comes, and tries
To kiss me, I 'll be maidenly and wise,
And say, Fie on you, sir!"

Philip Vernon, coming of a sudden through the hedge:

"Sweetheart, take this!
I 'll play rose-lover with you, till I kiss
You one red rose with blushes. He who brings
A galleon-freight of kisses, each with wings
Of gathered honor, cannot beggared be."

ELIZABETH VERNON. My love! my lord!

PHILIP VERNON.   One kiss from thee outweighs
    A hundred given. Not all love's usury,
    Not all the interest of unnumbered days,
    Can keep us even.

ELIZABETH VERNON.   There 's for ransom, see!
    Oh, I 'll be honest. Tell me of the fight.
    Indeed, I prayed for you both morn and night.
    Now, tell me of it. Did we hear aright?
    Hast seen the Queen?

PHILIP VERNON.   Aye, and she mocked me, too,
    Because these lands are cumbered, love, with you.

I had her pardon also. My Lord Grey
Takes more to kill him than most traitors may.

ELIZABETH VERNON. The packet reached the chancellor ?

PHILIP VERNON.   You did well
To send it. I have no long tale to tell.

ELIZABETH VERNON.
Sit near me, Philip. Now, the battle, pray!

PHILIP VERNON.
Oh, I 'll be brief; I 've other things to say.
We caught them in the Channel. Day by day
We hung about them, like bold dogs that tease
Great lumbering bullocks; left them at our ease,
Then bit again, until each bloody deck,
Mast, sail, and timber, shorn to shattered wreck,
Their cannon silent, helpless, overpowered,
Northward they drifted, and a storm that lowered
Broke on their ruin, pitiless and swift.
The gray fog closed about them like a pall;
The great seas, leaping, smote them, and the lift
Grew dark above them. One bleak funeral
They passed from sight of man. For us, we fled
To 'scape the storm's worst peril.
                          All is said
That may not till the morrow be delayed.

ELIZABETH VERNON.

    Ah, never day like this has England seen!
    Come, drink a cup to England and the Queen:
    I 'll cast my love within the bowl.

PHILIP VERNON.   That pearl

    Shall jewel every cup of life.

ELIZABETH VERNON.   Sweet Earl,

    Thy people grow impatient. Hark! the chimes
    Ring in their new lord, and these gladder times.